W9-CDF-577

WAITING
for the
WHALES

Written by
Sheryl McFarlane
Illustrated by
Ron Lightburn

Orca Book Publishers

ONCE, in a cedar-shingled cottage
on a bluff by the sea,
there lived a lonely old man.

In the evenings, he looked out over the water shimmering
with the last rays of light.

Often he saw bald eagles soaring,
majestic herons fishing,
and fat seals lounging on the rocky island
that would disappear at high tide.

But it was the orcas he longed to see. They travelled
up and down the strait in front of his home. Sometimes
he caught sight of them blowing in the distance.
They were so very far away that seeing them only
made him lonelier.

EVERY summer, the whales came in close to shore. They rubbed their enormous backs against the rocks of the island. And they feasted on salmon bound for spawning grounds up the creek that ran past his garden into the sea.

The old man watched the pod of orcas leap and breach and smack their tail flukes against the water. And as he stood on the bluff, his heart leapt with the whales below. It seemed to him that there was nothing more wonderful than these great mammals of the sea.

Each year as the whales departed, tears filled his eyes. He was alone again.

EVEN though his children had long since moved away, the old man continued to grow a huge garden, an enormous garden, a gigantic garden.

He tilled and he planted.

He weeded and he watered.

And when the crop was ready, he gave most of it away.

He was just one old man, and he couldn't eat everything he grew.

SOMETIMES during the long winter months, he collected oysters from the island that he could walk to at low tide. Or he dug clams on the sand spit. After each storm, which shook the great firs and bent the giant cedars up and down the coast, he collected seaweed for his garden.

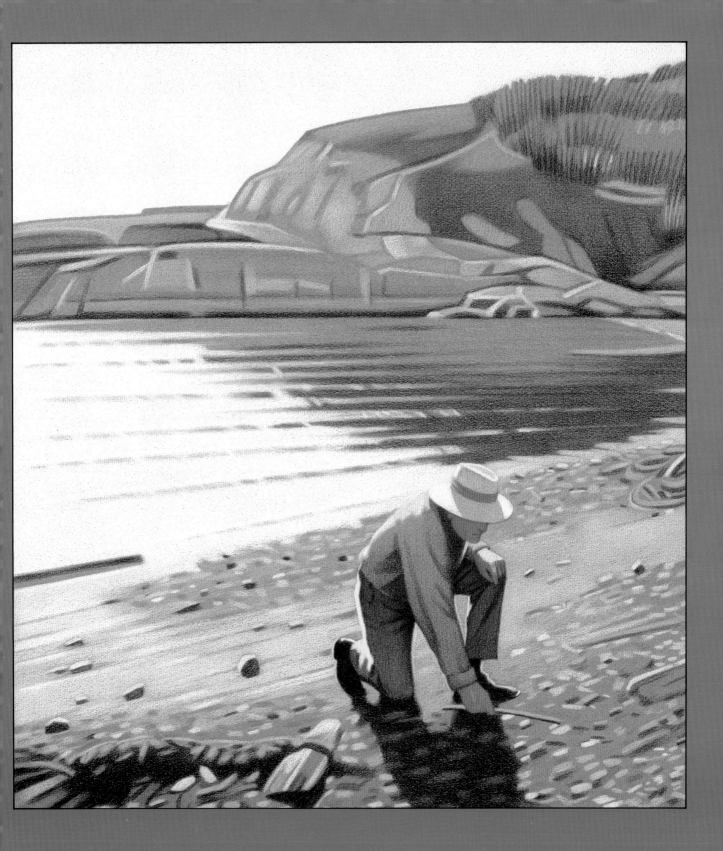

OTHER times he walked in the nearby woods watched over by the jagged peaks of the coastal range. He loved these woods. He had worked in them his whole life, and they had been his playground as a child long, long ago.

He knew each tree, each clearing, each trail and where it led.
He knew where to collect the best salal to send to florist shops in the city.
He knew where to gather watercress for his soups.
And he was always on the lookout for fallen logs, which could be sawed up for firewood to keep the chill of winter from his old bones.

But sometimes he just stared out at the fish boats that bobbed on the misty grey water, and waited for the orcas to return.

ONE crisp spring day, his daughter arrived unexpectedly. In one arm she held her bags, and in the other, a fat baby girl.

The old man grumbled something about noisy babies. But when he held the tiny infant, something deep within him stirred. And he remembered holding his own children when they were small.

WHEN he spotted the orcas that year, he carried his granddaughter to the water's edge and held her up so she could see. And although she didn't understand, he told her all about the whales that he had watched since he was small.

THE fat baby girl grew into a serious little girl,
a wild little girl,
a stubborn little girl.

She stuck to her grandfather like glue.

And although he grumbled, he took her everywhere.

In the garden they tilled and they planted.

They weeded and they watered.

And when the crop was ready, they gave most of it away (except for the raspberries, which the little girl loved best of all).

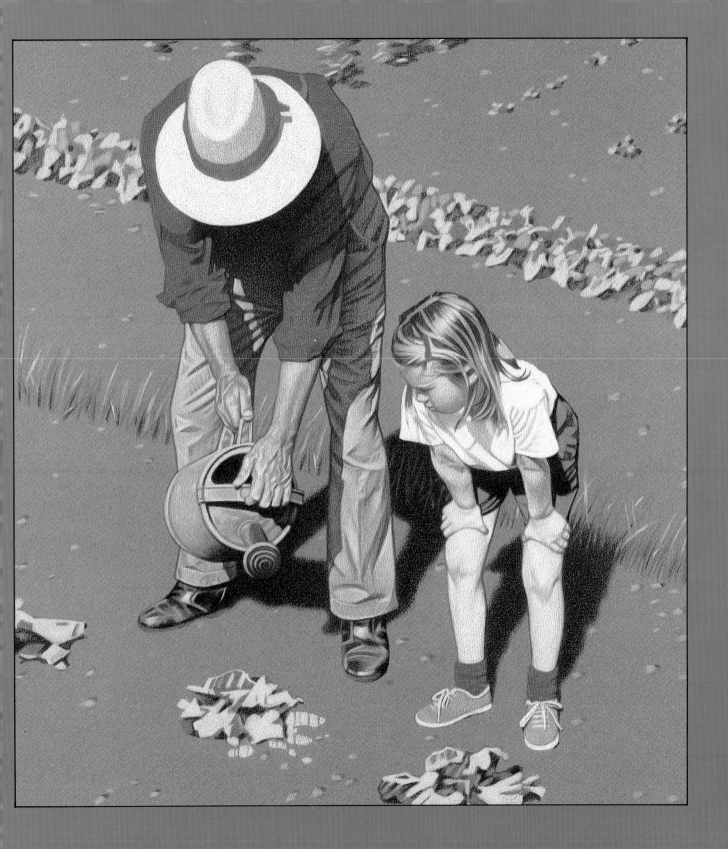

SOMETIMES during the long winter months, they collected oysters or dug clams. And after each storm they gathered seaweed for the garden.

Other times they walked in the woods.

The little girl learned each tree, each clearing, each trail and where it led.

She learned where to find the best salal patches and where to gather watercress for soups.

She learned to look for fallen logs which could be sawed into firewood to keep the chill of winter from her grandfather's old bones.

In the evenings, they watched the tugs with loaded barges inch down the coast. But it was the orcas that they waited for.

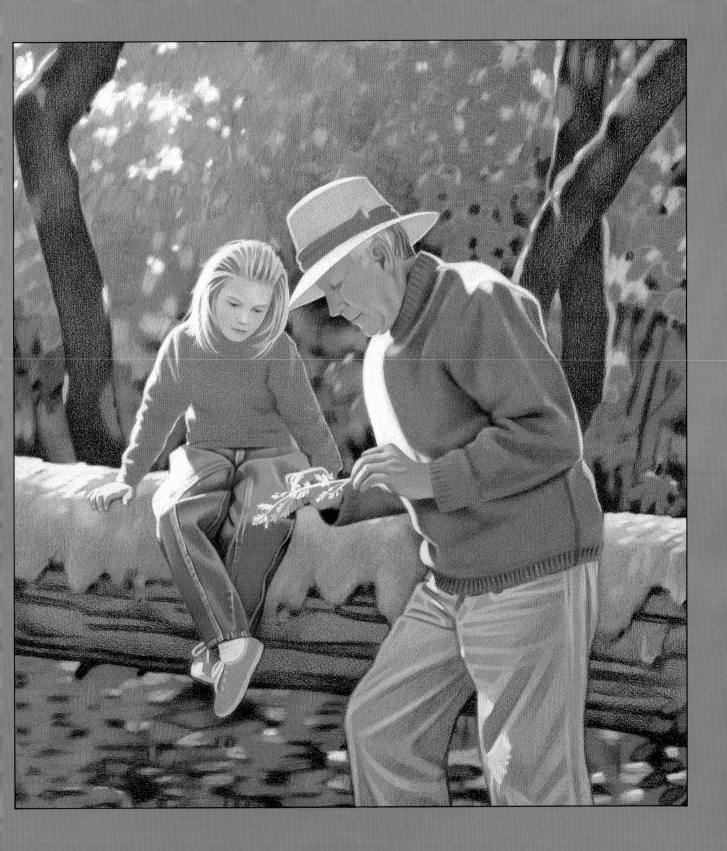

THEN one spring, the old man refused to till or to plant, to water or to weed. "It's time for me to rest," was all that he would say.

That year, mother and daughter tilled and planted the garden. They watered and they weeded, and when the crop was ready, they gave most of it away. They gathered salal and watercress and brought in the wood to keep the chill of winter from their bones.

THE old man helped them sometimes. But usually
he sat on the porch in front of his
cedar-shingled cottage
on the bluff by the sea.

He saw bald eagles soaring,
majestic herons fishing
and fat seals lounging on the rocky island
that would disappear at high tide. As he looked out
over the water shimmering with the last rays of light,
he waited for the orcas to return.

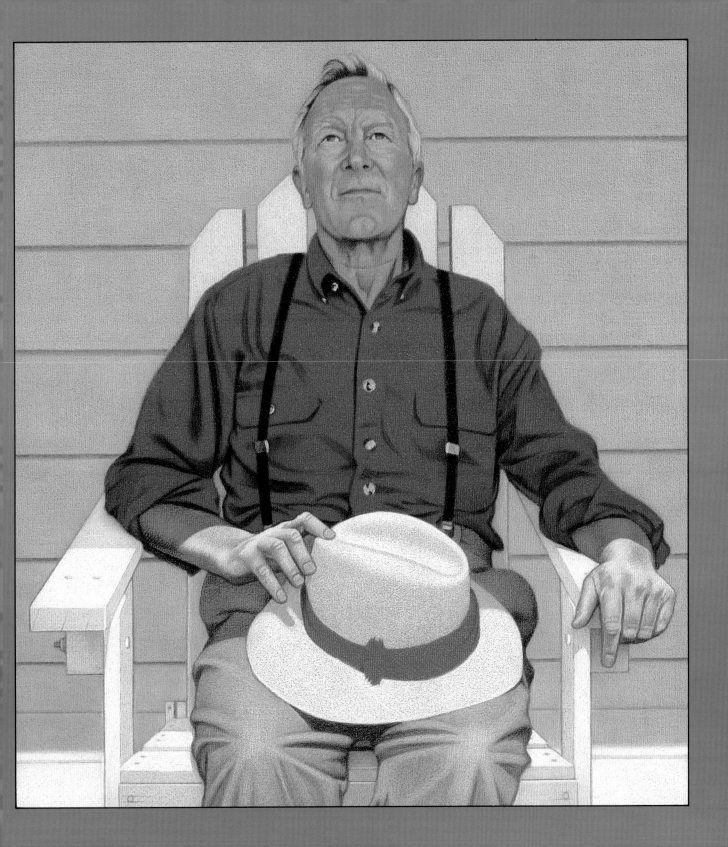

THE day the orcas came that summer, the old man died.

And when the little girl wept for her grandfather, her mother dried her tears. "Don't be sad, sweet girl. Your grandfather's spirit has gone to leap and swim with the whales."

MANY times that winter, mother and daughter looked out over the stormy grey water of the strait and waited for the orcas to return.

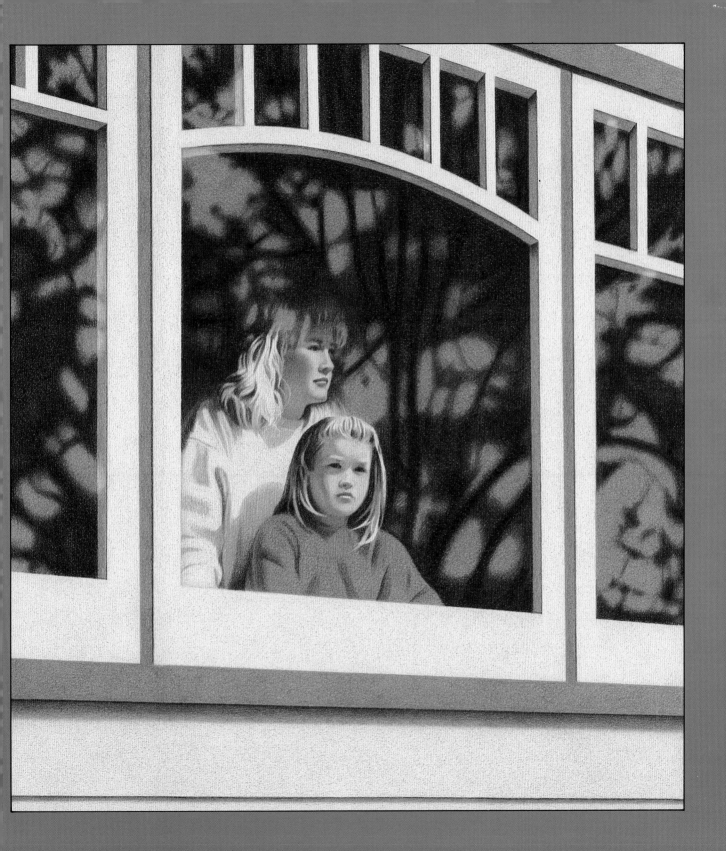

IT wasn't until summer that the little girl saw them next. One hot evening in July, her mother sent her to water the garden. Before she turned to climb the hill back to the house, she looked out toward the island. There they were. Orcas. Powerful flashes against the warm glow of golden water. But something was different. She sensed it right away. Some of the whales seemed to be hanging back.

MOMENTS later, the bay was filled with black dorsal fins cutting through the water. When the girl spotted a calf swimming between its mother and an old bull, a fierce cry of joy escaped her.

And right away, she flew up the hill to tell her mother.

To the bond between young and old;
in memory of Roy Padgett;
and in memory of my own grandfather, who lives
still in my heart.
With special thanks to my husband and family;
and to my editor, Ann Featherstone, for her insight
and tact.
S.M.

To Sam, with love.
Thanks to Bill, Allison, Devon and Andrea and a tip
of the hat to Claire.
R.L.

Text copyright © 1991 Sheryl McFarlane
Illustrations copyright © 1991 Ron Lightburn

All rights reserved.

Publication assistance provided by the Canada Council.

Orca Book Publishers
P.O. Box 5626, Stn. B
Victoria, B.C.
V8R 6S4

Design by Christine Toller and Ron Lightburn
Printed and bound in Hong Kong

10 9 8 7 6 5 4

Canadian Cataloguing in Publication Data

McFarlane, Sheryl, 1954–
Waiting for the whales

ISBN 0-920501-96-6

I. Lightburn, Ron.   II. Title.
PS8575.F36W3 1991   jC813'.54   C91-091543-1
PZ7.M32Wa 199